GWYDION
AND THE
FLYING WAND

Gwydion
and the
Flying Wand

Jenny Sullivan

For the Sullivan menfolk:
my adored husband Rob,
and the best father-in-law in the world, Bill,
with all my love.

J.S.

First Impression—2000

ISBN 1 85902 836 5

© Jenny Sullivan

Jenny Sullivan has asserted her right under the
Copyright, Designs and Patents Act, 1988,
to be identified as Author of this Work.

This book is published with the support of the
Arts Council of Wales.

Printed in Wales by
Gomer Press, Llandysul, Ceredigion

Chapter One

Merlin scratched his chin and pushed his spectacles up on his forehead. 'Drat!' he muttered. 'I can never find the beastly thing when I want it. Now, where on earth did I put it?'

Gwydion, Merlin's assistant, hid under the table and kept very quiet. The trouble – and this was the reason he was hiding – was that he knew EXACTLY what had happened to it (the thing Merlin was searching for), and if he reminded him, Merlin would certainly lose his temper. Again.

Merlin had lost his wand, which wasn't surprising, since Merlin had hurled it into the air in a fit of fury, because –

Because Gwydion had played a prank on him which involved a bucket of very cold water and Merlin's best starry robe. It was only a *small* bucket of water, Gwydion thought glumly. Can't he take a joke?

Well, Merlin obviously couldn't, because when the water had landed on his head, he was cross. And when his best robe (which he had worn especially that day because the King had asked him to lunch) had got soaked, and the lovely silver and purple colours had run, and then the robe had shrunk so small that it wouldn't fit him any more, he was furious.

Of course, Merlin knew exactly who had played the trick on him. It hadn't been hard for him to guess, because his ten-year-old assistant was rolling helplessly about on the floor, clutching his sides and laughing. Merlin had snatched up the nearest thing, which happened to be his wand, and chucked it at Gwydion. Fortunately, Gwydion always kept one eye on his teacher, whose bad temper was well known, and was able to dodge the wand, because if it had hit him, goodness knows what might have happened. He might have turned into a frog, for instance, or a slug, and he wouldn't have liked that at all.

So, in a way, Gwydion knew exactly what had happened to the wand, but where it was *right then,* ah, that was quite a different matter. The wand seemed to have disappeared completely. Being a magic wand, of course it sometimes had a bit of a mind of its own, and then all sorts of very strange things happened.

Merlin lifted the purple and yellow tablecloth and found Gwydion hiding beneath. 'You, boy!' he thundered. 'Where's my wand, eh? I distinctly remember chucking it at you. So where is it? What have you done with it?' He frowned, and his eyebrows (which were very bushy) got all tangled together, and by the time he'd found his comb (in the twenty-seventh pocket he looked in: his robe had at least 232 extremely useful pockets of different sizes) he had completely forgotten all about his wand, and went off to his turret for a tuna-fish sandwich to keep him going until lunchtime with the King.

Gwydion searched the turret room first, in case the wand had bounced off the wall and fallen behind the stuffed rhinoceros or the bats' nest (bat toenails were often used in Merlin's potions. These bats had the *shortest* toenails in the bat world, and were quite vain about it). There were a lot of dust-mice behind the rhinoceros, and the bats squeaked crossly, but the wand wasn't in either place. He looked behind the wardrobe where Merlin kept his clothes, and then inside it, as well. Merlin had a great many clothes, some of them very strange-looking, probably because they hadn't been invented yet. Merlin was like that: always popping into the future and bringing stuff back. He kept everything, just in case it came in useful one day (like the microwave, for instance, which would be WONDERFUL when someone invented electricity).

The trouble was, Gwydion knew perfectly well that sooner or later Merlin would remember that his wand was missing, and that it was all Gwydion's fault, and then he'd be in trouble again.

He tried to remember exactly where he'd been standing – well, rolling and laughing, anyway – when Merlin had thrown the wand. He scratched his head, and paced about a bit until he remembered. Ah, yes! He'd been *there* by the big globe of the world which had **BEWARE! HERE BE DRAGONS** written in big red letters all over the wiggly green blob that was Ynys Haf, (which would one day become known as Wales). Gwydion snorted. How ridiculous, writing it down like that! Everyone knew that Ynys Haf was full of dragons, but they weren't all dangerous, so you didn't need to beware of all of them. Some of them – the smaller sort – made lovely pets if they were captured straight out of the egg and well-trained. The bigger ones could be a bit unpredictable once they got over twelve metres tall. They didn't mean to do it, but sometimes they trod on people without noticing, and sort of squished them a bit, and they weren't very good at cutting their toe-nails, so they grew long and sharp and – well, I expect you can imagine the rest . . .

Anyway, Gwydion had been rolling about over there, and Merlin had been bellowing over by there, and so the wand must have sailed through the window in that wall there, and therefore – it must be down below somewhere! Simple!

Gwydion peered out of the window. It was a long way down, even though Merlin's workshop was only half-way up his tall tower. Right below the window was a blackberry bush. Gwydion's heart sank. Blackberries meant sharp thorns. Nevertheless, he put on his best walking boots, the ones with the hobnails and red laces, and went to look for the missing wand. He plodded down the stone spiral staircase to the garden and began to search.

Half an hour later, with a great many scratches and a mouth and fingers smeared with dark red blackberry juice (well, there was no use wasting the blackberries he'd found, was there?) Gwydion was quite sure that the wand was not in the bush. Had it taken it into its head to run away somewhere? Or perhaps disguise itself as something else? (It had done that once: it had been a duck for a fortnight, swimming about on a pond, and it was only when all the other ducks turned purple with green and yellow spots and began to bark, not quack, that Merlin realised where his missing wand was). That was one of the problems with magic: quite a lot of the stuff you had to use, like wands and spell-books and potions, often had quite determined little minds of their own, and occasionally did exactly what their little minds felt like doing!

Gwydion sat down on a large stone nearby, to think. He got up again immediately, because the stone gave his sit-upon a sort of electric shock, which could mean only one thing. Magic!

Rubbing the seat of his trousers, Gwydion stared at the stone. A stone had no right to be so magical, even in Ynys Haf, where there was magic everywhere. Stones usually needed a spell on them, or some close contact with something extremely magical to make them behave like that, and give a person a shock. He peered closer: yes, there it was. A faint trace of sparkle on the right side of the rock. That meant that Merlin's wand had bounced off the rock and shot off – where? Could be anywhere, Gwydion thought, and began to search.

Half an hour later he knew where the wand had gone. Not where it was, exactly, but where it had gone.

All over Ynys Haf there were special places. These places were Doors in Time. They didn't always look like doors – indeed, some of them looked like pairs of tall upright stones; some like holes in rocky walls, some like – well, just *strange* places in thin air. But they were all Doorways into Time. Some went forward in Time, some went back, but Time was where all the doorways led.

Gwydion had never travelled through a Time Door. Merlin kept telling him he was far too young and much too stupid to even think about going, so of course Gwydion thought about going quite often. About twice a day, in fact. He was that sort of boy. And here, right in front of him, was a Time Doorway with a sparkly smudge of magic *just inside the entrance*. What was a Magician's Assistant supposed to do? Ignore it?

Gwydion peered between the stone pillars. He couldn't see anything. He walked around the stones and peered through in the other direction. The space between the stones looked faintly fuzzy, but he couldn't see any trace of Merlin's wand between them. He took a deep breath. There was obviously nothing else for it but to walk through the Time Door to try to find Merlin's missing wand. He tried hard not to grin. Here was the perfect excuse to disobey Merlin's orders – and if he found the wand, he'd get away with it completely, because Merlin would be so pleased to have it back, he'd forget to be cross!

On the other hand, if he came back without it, Merlin would not be twice as cross. He'd probably be about fifty thousand times as cross, Gwydion thought glumly. He'd probably lose his temper so thoroughly that he might never get it back. He might turn Gwydion into a newt and use him in a spell. He might . . .

He might do all sorts of things, Gwydion thought, but NOT if I find the wand, right?

Chapter Two

Somewhere near Port Talbot, in the Other Wales, right around the time that Merlin's wand went missing, Betsan Price was walking on a small mountain. The sun was hot, and all around her loomed other small mountains: the Bwlch, the Graig, great rounded humps like giant mole-hills, all looking blue and faintly wobbly in the heat-haze. Far below, in the little village of Blaengwynfi little terraced houses rolled up and down its hilly streets. Betsan was entirely minding her own business when

CLUNK!

Something hard bashed her on the side of the head. 'Ouch!' she said (as most people do when they are hurt). She rubbed her head and looked around her, crossly, wondering if someone had thrown something at her. If they had, she'd have something to say. Downright dangerous, that was, chucking stuff at people. But there was no one about. Whatever it was seemed to have fallen from a clear blue sky. She'd read in the newspaper about bits dropping off aeroplanes, lumps of ice and stuff, but there was nothing at all lying around the mountain that looked in the least like a bit of an aeroplane or an overgrown ice-cube. She rubbed her head again, feeling the lump which was swelling up. She was going to have what her Grancher called "a nice little egg" there. When she took them away, her fingers felt wet. Aaargh! she thought, I'm bleeding to death! but when she looked at her fingers there was no sign of blood, only some sparkly stuff, like the glitter on a Christmas card, only better. She rubbed her fingers together, and jumped. Her fingers tingled. They felt the way they did when she folded clothes for Mam straight out of the tumble-drier. What was it called? Something electricity. Static electricity, that was it. It felt like a little tiny electric shock. Betsan sat down on the coarse mountain grass and wondered if the bump had muddled her brain. Perhaps she'd need to go to hospital to have her head X-rayed. Perhaps they'd make her stay in and she'd miss netball on Monday. That would be terrible, right? Not. Betsan was small, and she spent most of her games lessons trying to avoid getting bumped by the knees and elbows of the bigger kids in her class.

Then, close to her left foot, she saw a curious, oddly shaped wooden stick. It was thick at the bottom, about as thick as a medium sized banana, but straight, not bent like a banana. It got narrower at the other end and finished in a point. Around the middle were some peculiar carvings.

Betsan picked up the stick – and dropped it again, straight away. 'Ow!' she said, shaking her tingling hand. The ends of her fingers felt numb, as if she'd been holding ice cubes, and she looked at them. Her fingertips were covered in the same sparkly stuff that she had found on her bashed head. It was the stick that had fallen on her!

Carefully, using a wad of paper handkerchiefs she found in her jeans pocket, she picked up the stick. There was no tingle this time. The stick was very light, and yet the grass where she had dropped it was flattened into its long shape, as if an elephant had trodden it down, hard, into the earth. Betsan peered at the carvings. They seemed to be in the shape of letters, and it looked like Welsh in places, but still she couldn't understand it. The wood was blackened and looked old. She wondered what it was. It could be the leg of a very thin, ancient and rickety coffee table, or an old blackboard pointer, or a copper-stick like the one Mamgu kept in the outside *tŷ bach* from long ago, when she used to boil all her washing in a big copper boiler, and stir it and fish it out with the stick, not to burn her fingers. But now Mamgu had an electric washing machine, and the copper stick hung on the whitewashed wall, collecting cobwebs.

Betsan waved the stick around, and poked the pointed end into a clump of grass. She swished it at some nettles and chopped their heads off. Then, carrying the strange stick, she walked down the hill and into the valley.

The house where Betsan and her Mam and Grancher lived half-way down a long, steep hill, lined each side with rows of joined-up terraced houses, where everyone knew everyone else. Mamgu (who was Dad's Mam) always said that if someone up the top of the hill sneezed, everyone down the bottom of the hill caught a cold, which was her way of saying that everyone knew everyone else.

Grancher was Mam's Dad and because Betsan's Dad worked abroad, Grancher lived with them to keep Mam and Betsan company, and to take care of the garden, which was full of vegetables and fruit and butterflies, which were lovely, and caterpillars and slugs, which weren't.

Betsan pushed open the front door calling 'I'm home, Granch!' Mam was at work and wouldn't be back until tea-time. Grancher didn't answer; he was probably taking a nap. He was nearly eighty, so he got tired during the day, even though he wouldn't ever admit it. He always said he was 'just resting his eyes,' although he sometimes snored so loudly that the cat would jump off his lap and go and sit under the apple tree at the end of the garden. Betsan tiptoed upstairs, past Grancher's door, and put the strange stick in her bedroom. She decided to keep it to herself for a while, to see if she could work out what it was.

There was a note from Mam stuck to the fridge with a Snoopy magnet.

It said

Bets,
Sausage, egg and chips for tea. Please peel 3 large spuds, check the hen-house and see if there's any raspberries ripe.

Love Mam.

PS You won't find the raspberries in the hen-house!

Har, har, Betsan thought. Her Mam had a very weird sense of humour, sometimes. She opened the back door and got some potatoes from the sack in the shed, peeled them and put them in water so that they wouldn't turn black. Then she went down to the far end of the garden where the speckled hens pecked and poked, and lifted the lid of their nestbox, feeling around in the straw. She found five brown eggs, and carried them carefully back into the kitchen. Then she took a plastic bowl from the cupboard and went down the end of the garden to the raspberry canes. She parted the dark leaves gently, looking for the fat red berries, and noticed that, despite peeling the potatoes (and washing her hands first and rinsing and drying them after) the sparkly stuff was still on her fingertips. She picked steadily, gathering all the ripe ones, and then had to hunt a bit harder to find enough for them all to eat for tea. By mistake, she picked a raspberry that was hard and green.

'Rats!' she muttered. She hated to waste even one berry: they were her favourite, especially with raspberry ripple ice cream. She rolled the berry between her fingertips, where the sparkly stuff was. And then she gasped.

Where there had been an unripe, sour, hard berry there was now a dark red, luscious fruit bursting with juice! She stared. How could that happen? Could she have been mistaken? No, definitely not. That raspberry had been hard and green. While she thought about it, she popped the raspberry into her mouth. It was possibly – no, definitely – the most delicious raspberry she had ever eaten in her whole life!

Betsan examined her fingertips. Since picking that raspberry, some of the sparkle had worn off, but there was a little left on her middle finger. Choosing a thoroughly green, small, hard and totally unripe berry, Betsan rubbed it gently with the glittery stuff. She watched in amazement as the raspberry swelled and gradually changed colour, turning ripe and juicy before her eyes.

Thoughtfully, she picked and ate it. Like the first one, it was absolutely delicious, the most raspberriest raspberry ever.

There was something seriously weird going on!

Chapter Three

Gwydion took a deep breath. Now that he had made the decision to risk the Time Door, he was beginning to feel just a little nervous. Sort of quaky round the ankles, and thump-ish around the heart. Suppose he went through the door and something large, with teeth, decided he would make a delicious breakfast with some tomato sauce and baked beans, and – Gwydion decided he'd worry about that if it happened.

But it was a serious matter, this walking through Time Doors. Goodness only knew *when* he'd be. Or where, he thought. Still, it was an Adventure, and Gwydion was always in favour of Adventures! *I am not scared* he told himself fiercely. *I am Gwydion Dragonson, Apprentice to Great (but bad-tempered) Merlin, and I AM NOT SCARED*.

But Merlin's wand was missing, and if Gwydion didn't find it there'd be a problem. Probably a painful problem for Gwydion, if Merlin had anything to do with it.

He definitely had to go. There was nothing else for it. Gwydion looked at the fuzzy air between the two great side-by-side stones. This Door had a third stone laid across the top, and that somehow made it look twice as sinister. Now that the opportunity of going through a Door had arrived, was Gwydion going to chicken out? He scowled and put his shoulders back. He might be scared, but he wasn't a coward.

Taking a deep breath he stepped inside the Door. It was strange, because it shouldn't really have been any different inside the stones than it was outside. But it was. Once he was between the stones, right in the middle of that fuzzy air, everything changed.

He hadn't known what to expect – but it certainly wasn't this! Instead of daylight just a step or two ahead, there was a long tunnel with just a faint glow in the distance. Gwydion started walking towards the glow.

And then the wind began. Not just a gentle summer breeze, mind, but quite a strong wind, gusting into his face, shoving rough fingers into his hair and making it stand on end. It got stronger and stronger, so strong that he had to bend forward, leaning into the powerful force. It was so strong that it was blowing him backwards, so strong that he had to hang on to the rocky walls not to be blown right out of the Time Door like a dead leaf from a tree. The wind howled and blew and pushed against him like a live thing, like a giant hand pressing against his chest. He had to keep going forward.

Gwydion knew enough about Time Doors to know that it was horribly dangerous to try to turn round whilst going through one. He could get stuck in Time for centuries if he tried to turn back when he was half way. He might be stuck there forever, until he was an old, old man, older than Merlin, who must be at least seven thousand five hundred and forty-two.

Then, just as he was beginning to think he couldn't hang on one second longer, and the howling wind was going to sweep him backwards out of the tunnel, it dropped. Suddenly. Gwydion, who had been leaning forward and pushing with all his might against the power of the wind, shot through the other side of the Time Door, the way someone leaning on a door will shoot through if it is opened suddenly. He landed flat on his face.

Luckily, he was in a lonely place on top of a small mountain, bare except for the familiar upright stones, and not in the middle of a bustling market place where he would certainly have been noticed, arriving from nowhere and skidding forward on his nose like that. He sat up, brushed the dust from his tunic and picked some grass out of his hair. He had some dirt in his mouth as well, so he spat that out and looked around him. He was surrounded by small mountains, and he could hear a river somewhere near. He stood up, and stared.

Down below him in the valley were some of the strangest dwellings he'd ever seen! Back home, only very rich people lived in stone houses, Kings and people like that, and people like him and Merlin lived with them as guests. Everyone else lived in wooden houses, or huts made of mud and sticks and stuff. But here it seemed that everyone was very rich, because the valley held some of the longest long-houses he'd ever seen, marching up and down the hill in great curving lines. Even from so high up Gwydion could see how huge they were. Very rich and powerful kings must live in those stone long-houses.

Gwydion decided it would be an extremely good idea to find Merlin's wand and go back to Ynys Haf, quick, before the king of this place learned that he was here and locked him in a dungeon or made him fight a dragon or something. Kings had a habit of doing stuff like that. It was what Kings did for fun, probably. Gwydion had noticed that sometimes Kings' amusements were uncomfortable – for other people, that is.

Gwydion began to search the mountain-top for the wand, carefully walking up and down all its sides and looking so hard his eyes began to ache. He discovered a baby rabbit drowsing contentedly, and almost stepped on a sleepy adder basking in the sun. It squirmed away as soon as it woke up and felt the vibration of his footsteps, but there was no sign of the wand. At last he sank down on the grass, hot and tired and beginning to get cross. He'd hoped he could just pop through the Door, spot the wand and take it back as quickly as he'd come.

He should have known better. Nothing was ever easy where he was concerned. The wand had probably decided it needed a holiday, that it was getting fed up with being hurled at student wizards, and was now on the other side of the world, sunbathing, or practising being an elephant or something.

And then Gwydion saw the mark, right next to his foot. It was a long, thin mark, wider at one end than the other, and so deeply pressed into the ground that whatever had made it must have been made either of lead or of the special sort of wood that only magic wands are made of. He groaned. It had been here, then. But where was it now? Below him the valley with its strange, long, long, long-houses waited, shining in the sun.

Gwydion gazed down the valley. He really didn't want to go down there. This certainly wasn't Ynys Haf any more: he didn't know where it was, but it was a strange place and the comforting sight of Merlin's tower was nowhere about.

He decided that it would be safer to wait until dark, when people would be less likely to see him, before venturing down. He could use the shadows to hide in, then. He followed the sound of running water until he found the stream that wound down the hill and into the valley, had a drink, and lay down under a tree to wait. But the day was hot, and Gwydion had had a long, tiring day searching for Merlin's missing wand, and of course . . .

He fell asleep.

He woke up, suddenly. A monster was standing over him. He could feel its hot, smelly breath on his face, and something sharp was digging into his side. Gwydion kept his eyes tightly shut. He knew, beyond any doubt, that a dragon had found him. He could feel its sharp claws cutting into his tunic. He had come all this way, battled against the winds of the Time Door, just to be eaten alive by a dragon. Probably without any tomato sauce or baked beans, either, he thought miserably. He opened his mouth to shriek, and then the monster said 'Baaaaa!' and Gwydion realised that the dragon was only a sheep trying to share his resting-place under the tree. He felt extremely silly.

'Get off, sheep,' Gwydion said crossly, and pushed the sharp hoof away. The sheep wandered off into the darkness, bleating mournfully, and Gwydion stood up, stretching to take the stiffness out of his bones, glad that no one he knew had been there to see him terrified of a sheep. Half way through his stretch, he glanced down at the valley below, and stared. *All the long-houses had great necklaces of lights outside them!* They stretched in long strings up and down, and the valley glowed yellow in the glare. Gwydion was used to fiery torches being used outside the castle where he lived: they were stuck in holders on the walls and they certainly helped to stop people tripping over the barrels and boxes of stuff that were always lying around. But these torches didn't flicker like flame, they burned with a steady orange glow that was scary. Even Merlin couldn't make a torch burn as steadily as these torches and not flicker at all! (Maybe he hasn't ever tried, though, Gwydion thought, not wanting to be disloyal to his teacher. He probably could if he put his mind to it).

Gwydion really didn't want to go down the mountain and into the valley towards those eerie lights. And then an owl hooted close to his ear, and he jumped with fright and decided he didn't particularly want to stay up on the mountain, either! His heart was still thumping after the sheep-dragon episode. Altogether, Gwydion decided that he would much rather be back in Ynys Haf. But that would mean Merlin still wouldn't have his wand, and then he'd be in trouble again, especially since he'd disobeyed Merlin's orders and passed through a Time Door. He might just as well stay here and get on with finding Merlin's wand.

Chapter Four

By the time Betsan's Mam came in from work, the chip-pan was sitting on the stove, the raspberries had been washed, the sausages were arranged in neat pink rows under the grill, and the table was set for tea. Betsan's strange stick was hidden under her bed, and Granch had stopped (loudly) resting his eyes and was reading the *"South Wales Echo"* instead.

Mam sat down and kicked off her shoes. She worked in a shop in Port Talbot all day, and her feet often hurt her. 'I think I'll have a nice bath after tea,' she sighed, massaging her ankles. 'And maybe an early night. It's been a horrible day in work. All the customers seemed to be cross for some reason.'

'Shall I cook tea, Mam?' Betsan suggested.

Mam grinned. 'Since it's chips, *dim diolch, cariad!'*

'Just because the chip pan caught fire last time doesn't mean it'll happen again, Mam,' Betsan protested.

'It wouldn't have happened last time if you hadn't had your nose stuck in a book!' Granch said. 'I'm all for reading, but not when you're supposed to be cooking my tea. Took me four days to redecorate the downstairs! All that smoke!'

'Anyway,' Mam got up and padded barefoot into the kitchen, 'I'll cook it, you wash up, O.K.?'

They had just finished eating the raspberries (none of which tasted as wonderful as the "glittery" ones had) when the back door opened. A small, freckly face wearing a large pair of glasses appeared round it.

'Hiya,' the face said, 'Anyone home? 'S me.'

'Hello Smee,' Granch said. 'Where's Captain Hook and Peter Pan?'

'Ha ha, Granch. Not funny. The name's Clint,' the visitor said, scowling.

His name wasn't really Clint, it was Maldwyn, but he hated his name and about once a month chose a new one for himself. This month's was Clint, and last month's had been Jason, and goodness knows, Betsan thought, what it would be next month. She had a hard job keeping up with him, sometimes. But he was her best friend, and had been since they were in playgroup together, when they had had a big fight just once, over a sit-on tractor, and whose turn it was to ride it, and then not bothered any more.

'Clint, is it?' Granch said, and cocked his eyebrow. 'Thought it was Jason.'

'Nah,' Maldwyn said. 'Went off that. Hey, Granch! Did you see the Cardiff/Llanelli game on telly last night? Brilliant, wasn't it?' Maldwyn was rugby mad. One of his Uncles had been capped for Wales, and it was what Maldwyn wanted to do more than anything else. Of course, Betsan thought, he'd have to grow a bit, first. A lot, actually.

Granch folded his newspaper. 'Fell asleep half way through. Rugby's not what it was in my day. I remember, during the seventies, when Gareth Edwards and Barry John were playing . . .'

'Anyway,' Maldwyn said quickly, not wanting to let Granch get started on one of his stories, even a rugby one, 'is Betsan coming out tonight?'

'I don't know,' Mam replied, glancing at Betsan. 'Is she?'

'Go on,' Granch said. 'I'll do the washing up. I've been resting my eyes all afternoon.'

'Thanks, Granch.'

Outside, the day was still warm, although the sun was going down behind the mountain. Betsan and Maldwyn raced each other down the hill (Maldwyn won), each in turn grabbing the lamp-post at the bottom so that they wouldn't shoot out onto the main road, and walked more slowly up the hill towards the recreation ground behind the school, which was closed for the weekend. It always looked strange, all shut up like that, especially in the summer holidays, which began in just over a week. Betsan and Maldwyn would be in Year Six in September, and then – gulp! – Betsan thought. Da-da-daaaa! The Comprehensive!

She pushed that thought away. Plenty of time to

worry about that next year. They reached the Rec and chose swings side by side. Betsan liked to stand on hers, swooping the red plastic seat high into the sky until the chain snapped alarmingly at the top of the swing. Then she sat down and allowed the motion to die down, enjoying the cool wind on her face. She closed her eyes and thought about the strange stick. She decided not to tell Maldwyn about it yet. Not until she'd had a chance to think about it a bit.

The chimes of the ice-cream van echoed down the valley. 'Come on Mal – er, Clint,' she said. 'Fancy an ice-cream? I've got just enough money for two Fab-o-Kools.'

They queued with five or six other kids until they were served, then ambled down the path licking their ice-cream cones. Maldwyn slurped his happily. Neither of them noticed the two larger boys standing in the shade of a tree until it was too late. One of them grabbed Maldwyn by the scruff of the neck.

'Leave him alone, Dwayne Morris!' Betsan said fiercely, and rushed forward, intending to kick the big boy hard on the shins to make him let go of Maldwyn. But the other boy, whom everyone called Crusher, grabbed her, twisted her arm painfully behind her back and stopped her. She struggled, but Crusher was much bigger than she was, and she was helpless.

'Well, if it isn't Skinny Mal-der-wyn Four-eyes!'

Dwayne sneered, and, still holding Maldwyn's T-shirt, grabbed his other hand and shoved the ice-cream into his face. 'There, face cream for Mal-der-wyn Four-eyes. Make you pretty!' And the two big boys ran away, laughing.

It wasn't the first time Dwayne and Crusher had ambushed them. They always picked on kids smaller than themselves, and quite often on Maldwyn. Usually he and Betsan kept their eyes well peeled for the two bullies, but this time they had been preoccupied with their ice-creams.

Maldwyn took off his messed-up glasses, got a big hanky out of his shorts and wiped his face. There was ice-cream in his hair and all over his cheeks, which were very red. Betsan didn't know what to say. Maldwyn was just the sort of boy who always got bullied. She couldn't understand it. He was lovely; she'd never heard him say an unkind word about anyone. He lived on his own with his Mam: he didn't seem to have a Dad, and Betsan had never asked why. After all, she didn't have a Dad either, except when he came home from abroad, and it was nobody's business but hers and her Mam's.

Maldwyn was skinny, and short, and – even Betsan had to admit it – sort of funny-looking. His ears stuck out, and his glasses seemed too big, and his knees were knobbly, and he didn't wear the same sort of clothes as all the other kids. But he was kind and he was her friend.

Betsan resolved that, somehow or other, she would make it up to him. She didn't know how, but she would.

'Clint,' she said, determinedly, 'lets go back to my house. I'll ask Mam if we can get a video from the corner shop and see if Granch will let us watch it in his room.'

Maldwyn put his smeary glasses back on and tossed the remnants of his ice-cream into a waste bin. 'Nah,' he said, not looking at her. 'Nah, thanks. I think I'll go home. Mam's on her own. I'll keep her comp'ny.'

Betsan watched him walk down the road, his thin shoulders hunched. Tears prickled at the back of her eyelids. She felt very helpless.

Chapter Five

It was much harder than Gwydion had expected, walking down the mountain in the dark. He followed the splashing sound of the stream downhill, knowing that eventually it would lead him to the long-house kingdom. But he kept stumbling over roots and stones and tussocks of grass, because, strangely, seeing was much more difficult than being in the dark usually was. Usually, once a person's eyes got used to the dark, they could see quite well, but the orange lights shining up from the valley only made the mountainside seem even darker. At last, bruised and out of breath, Gwydion arrived at the foot of the mountain. The stream promptly disappeared into a hole in the ground with a hollow, sloshing noise, but it had served its purpose and brought Gwydion down to the long-houses.

Keeping close to a high wall, he crept down the hill beside one of the buildings. The ground felt strange under his feet, and he realised that the mountain grass had given way to hundreds and hundreds of flat flagstones. How enormously rich this king must be! All these flagstones, and out in the open, too! Not even inside under the protective roof of a great hall! They fitted so closely together that there were hardly any gaps between them, forming a sort of ledge, and then there was a smooth, flat surface which looked like beaten earth, except that it was blacker and harder. Gwydion tested it with his foot. It was as hard as iron! Beside the flagstone ledge, in the strange long-house, there were rows of windows made of fine glass, which proved that the person who owned this place was very rich indeed. Only very rich people in Ynys Haf had glass windows: everyone else had wooden shutters or leather curtains to keep out the rain and wind, which made the huts very dark inside. But in these long-houses, curtains of many different colours covered the glass windows on the inside, and in chinks between some of them he could see bright, steady white lights, much too bright for candles.

And then he came to a window that had its curtains open. Carefully, he dropped down beneath the level of the window-sill, and crept past. When he was safely on the other side, he flattened himself against the wall, and craned his neck to see inside. What he saw almost stopped his breath!

There were some *tiny people, trapped in a small, square box sitting on a stand on the floor!* Three of them, sitting in tiny chairs, not looking out of the box, but talking to each other. Gwydion stared. They didn't look like the *tylwyth teg,* the fairies that haunted Ynys Haf's woods and hillsides. They looked like real people, but they were so tiny, and dressed in such strange clothes. The two men had bits of brightly coloured cloth dangling round their necks, and strange open-fronted dark tunics with collars, and the lady – well, her skirt was so short Gwydion could see her *knees!* That was indecent, that was! No lady ever showed her *ankles*, let alone her knees.

At this moment Gwydion decided it would be a good idea to take himself off somewhere else. He didn't want to get captured by the king who ruled this strange land, and turned into a little person and be put in a box for ever and ever! Especially not with ladies with their ankles showing. He turned around and began to run. He stepped off the ledge and onto the hard black earth, and ran. The road – for this was what it had to be, even though it was quite unlike the often muddy earth roads where Gwydion lived – eventually met and crossed another road at a place where the long-houses bent round a corner. This new road was just as hard and black, and had a pattern of spaced white lines written down the middle of it, and it wound its way downhill and uphill in the other direction, as far as Gwydion could see. Of course, if he'd been wise, he would have stopped, waited, looked to see what was round the corner, but he wanted to get away from that dreadful box full of captive people, prisoners of the awful king.

Then, suddenly, a monster with a terrible honking voice like an enormous dragon, and eyes that flashed like a hundred suns, was chasing him down the middle of the road. Gwydion took one look at the fearful thing bearing down on him, shrieked with terror, and ran. He could hear the monster growling and snarling behind him, and heard its deafening blaring roar. He could feel it getting closer. He knew it would catch him and eat him. And it moved so fast! A monster that big should make the ground shake with its passing, but apart from its roar, it was silent. He couldn't even tell how close it was!

Then Gwydion saw the wooden fence. Now, if there was one thing that Gwydion was good at, it was climbing fences in a hurry. Especially fences belonging to farmers with trees full of ripe apples.

Well, there were no farmers or apple-trees about – but Gwydion shot over the fence as if he were on springs, arriving on the other side out of breath and with his heart hammering like the blacksmith's anvil.

It was dark on the other side of the fence, away from the glare of the awful orange lights and the glowing eyes of the monster, and it took a while for Gwydion's eyes to get used to the darkness. He slid down the fence until he was sitting with his back against it, and tried to get his breath back. His chest hurt, he had a stitch in his side, and he was puffing and panting like a fat old man. Dragons were bad enough, but the monsters in this Time were twice as terrifying as any monster in his own, and there were some extremely nasty ones back then, with bad habits like biting people's heads off and roasting people alive with one big huff. He held his breath to listen, but the roaring noise had died away, and the monster didn't seem to be looking for him. He sighed with relief, and began to get up. Although the sky had a curious orangey glow from the torches-that-didn't-flicker, this side of the fence was very dark and full of shadows, and he didn't like being there at all. He pulled himself up to look over the fence, to make sure that the roaring, honking monster had gone.

And then from out of the darkness behind him, he heard a low, savage growl. Very slowly Gwydion let himself slide back down the fence, and stood very still, with his eyes squinched shut and his nose pressed against the wood. Had the monster circled round and crept up behind him? Slowly, slowly, he turned round and opened his eyes – and sighed with relief. Creeping out of the shadows, its ears flat against its head, its lips drawn back from sharp white teeth, was a large, powerful black dog. Its head was low between its shoulders, and the massive body was tensed, ready to spring at Gwydion's throat.

Whew! Gwydion thought. *What a relief! Only a dog.* A dog he could cope with, no problem. He smiled, holding out his hand. 'Hello, boy!' he said, 'good boy. Come on, then!'

The dog didn't understand that Gwydion was trying to make friends, because next thing, it launched itself like an arrow, snarling horribly, its teeth flashing in the dim light.

'Don't be silly!' Gwydion said crossly, and slapped the dog across the nose with a very small spell. He knew quite a few of those, certainly enough to cope with a savage dog. Merlin was teaching him, bit by bit, how to do magic.

The dog's nose fizzed, and it stopped in mid-leap and tried to look at it, only managing to go cross-eyed and trip over its paws. It sat bolt upright on the ground and looked bewildered. It stared at its nose, then at Gwydion, and, deciding that the fizzy-nose problem was nothing but its imagination, crouched to spring again.

Gwydion sighed. This time the spell was a little stronger, and the dog yelped and sneezed. It wasn't hurt, but it was extremely surprised. At last it realised that Gwydion was responsible for what was happening to its nose. It whined softly, and stopped snarling.

'That's better,' Gwydion said sternly. 'Haven't you been taught any manners, dog?' The dog whined, and sneezed again. 'Come on, boy,' Gwydion said, holding out his hand. Slowly, the dog crept up and sniffed Gwydion's hand. Then he put out a long pink tongue and licked it. Gwydion put his hand on the dog's head and concentrated, hard. He popped an idea into the dog's brain.

'There. Now, no more nonsense.' And Gwydion knelt down and rubbed the dog behind the ears and on its chest. The dog tried to wash Gwydion's face, completely forgetting that a few minutes ago he had been determined to bite this strange person, very hard.

'Good boy. Now,' Gwydion read the name on the dog's collar, 'Now, Fang, do you want to stay here, or are you coming with me?'

The dog made it perfectly clear (by sticking firmly at Gwydion's heels) that he now considered himself Gwydion's dog, and that was the end of the matter. Gwydion looked around the yard. The sky was getting lighter, and all around him he could see huge piles of strange metal objects of all shapes and sizes. He recognised a few dented old pots and cauldrons with holes in them, but that was all.

As dawn approached, Gwydion saw that there was a gate set in the fence, and unlatched it. Looking carefully up and down outside to make sure no one was coming, he and Fang crept out into the early morning.

Chapter Six

Betsan hadn't slept very well. She was very angry about what had happened to Maldwyn, and that kept her awake for a long time. She spent ages lying in her dark bedroom thinking up all sorts of revenge on Dwayne and Crusher (like boiling them in treacle or tying them to the rugby posts up on the Rec and letting Neil Jenkins kick a rugby ball at them). She vowed that one day – one day, honest – she would think of some way of getting back at them.

She was also still puzzled by the raspberry business, although she was certain the strange stick thing (or at least the glittery stuff that came off it) had something to do with it. She woke up during the night and saw that there was an eerie glow coming from under her bed. She rolled over and peered, cautiously. It was a stick-shaped eerie glow. Maybe the thing had dropped off an alien space-ship! Maybe any minute a seven-metre-tall bug with sticking-out eyes and waving antennae would burst through the bedroom door and demand its stick back! She didn't like that thought very much, and it took her ages to get back to sleep. She was woken again by the sound of a car horn, and the noise of someone – it sounded like a boy – screaming. *Hope it's Dwayne and Crusher* she thought drowsily. *Maybe the alien's gone after them instead . . .*

The house creaked, and once she thought she heard the alien growling outside her door, but when she calmed down and listened properly, she realised it was only Granch, snoring.

Next morning she left the stick under the bed and went down to breakfast. Luckily, the stick didn't glow in the daylight so Mam wouldn't notice it if she came into the room. Although it was Saturday, she had jobs to do for Mam, who was at work again, before she could go out and see who was hanging around the Rec this morning. With any luck there would be a rugby game going on, and Maldwyn might be up there. Despite the fact that he was small and wore glasses, he kept on trying to get on a team. He probably didn't have a hope, not even of getting on the school rugby team. He was too small, and although he could run fast, all the other players towered over him. After his Uncle Gethin had played for Wales about a million years ago, he had given Maldwyn his old red Wales shirt. He wore it as often as he could, and though his Mam washed it and it was always clean, it was getting very tatty and one day he would have to stop wearing it or it might drop off him. Granch said it was only the moths holding hands that kept it together! Betsan had laughed at this, but Maldwyn hadn't.

She hoped Maldwyn would be at the Rec, but somehow she doubted it. She had a feeling he would lie low for a bit, until he began to forget about the bullies. He always acted as though it was his own fault when someone picked on him, when it wasn't, almost as if he was ashamed of getting bullied. But he'd forget it after a while, and things would go on exactly as before, until the next time. *Only you don't ever honestly forget about being bullied*, she thought, *the horrible feeling of it was always with you, somehow.* A strange thought struck her. Perhaps the way Maldwyn kept changing his name meant something. Perhaps he knew that the person called "Maldwyn" would always get bullied, but a "Clint", or a "Jason" or a – what was the other name he'd had recently? Oh yes, "Brad", that was it. Perhaps a "Brad" wouldn't be bullied the way a Maldwyn was ... Trouble was, whatever his name was, he'd always be little and skinny, with knobbly knees and glasses.

But before she could go and look for Maldwyn by any name at all, there was the clean washing to peg on the line, runner beans to pick for dinner, and potatoes to scrub ready for baking in the oven. When she'd done all that, and taken Granch a cup of tea in bed (he looked so funny with his hair sticking up on end, without his teeth, which were sitting in a little pink plastic box in the bathroom), then she was free to go and enjoy the day. But before she left, she went into her room and fetched the strange stick. She found her winter gloves and put one on her right hand so that she could pick it up without getting a shock. She wasn't sure how to carry it, but she knew she wanted to take it with her. Then she noticed that there was a small hole bored in the top, and she found a piece of string in the kitchen drawer (the one Mam called her "busy drawer" because everything lying around got chucked into it, so it was always untidy). She threaded the string through the hole, and tied it onto the belt of her jeans. Then she pushed the stick (carefully!) down her jeans so that it lay flat against her leg. She did it slowly, carefully in case she got a shock, but she didn't. There was just the cold, hard feeling of the stick against her skin, so she took off the glove, and gritting her teeth, she dabbed her finger on the handle end. There was no tingle! Perhaps the stick was getting used to her . . .

Now that, she thought to herself, is *totally* ridiculous! As if an old stick could "get used to" anyone! It was a stick, that was all. O.K., it was old, and carved, and she couldn't imagine where it had come from, but it was just a stick . . .

But was it? She could feel it, rubbing gently against her bare leg, as she walked up the hill towards the playing fields. She called in at Mrs Davies's corner shop on the way, because Granch had given her a pound to spend. She chose some chocolate to share with Maldwyn/Clint if he was around, and handed over her money. There wasn't much change from the pound, but she slipped it into the pocket next to the stick. She put the chocolate in the other pocket. She hadn't walked very far when she noticed that her pocket, the one with the sweets in, felt strange. She stopped, and fished out the chocolate. Her pocket still felt odd, and she put her hand in again. And pulled out more chocolate. And when she'd done that, there was even more chocolate. That was impossible. Had Mrs Davies given her extra, by mistake? Couldn't have. Betsan had held the sweets, and Mrs Davies had taken the money. Betsan fished in her other pocket for the change, to count it, to make sure she had the right money. She pulled out a handful of change – *and four more bright new pound coins!*

Something very weird was happening. And it had to be something to do with the stick. First the raspberries, then the chocolate, and now the money. What next?

She soon found out. There was a rugby game going on up at the playing field, and Maldwyn was waiting for her, wearing his red rugby jersey with the three white feathers on. The jersey was huge and up close, Betsan could see that it looked as if a family of moths had had several good dinners and a great many breakfasts from the back. Two of the buttons were missing from the collar as well, and there was a huge hole in one of the sleeves.

'Hiya, Maldwyn!' Betsan said, offering him one of the multiplying bars of chocolate.

'Elliott,' Maldwyn/Clint/Jason mumbled with his mouth full.

'Right. Elliott now, is it?' Betsan raised her eyes to the sky in exasperation. 'I sometimes wish you'd pick a name and stick with it.'

'No you don't,' Maldwyn said, 'you'd get bored if I did.'

'Ha!' Betsan retorted, shoving him gently with the side the stick was hidden. Then she stopped, and blinked. Were her eyes playing tricks on her? 'Your rugby shirt!' she said. 'What's happened?'

'What?'

'Look at it, Maldwyn!'

Maldwyn looked down at himself, and his mouth fell open. His ancient, tattered, moth-eaten rugby shirt looked brand new. It was so red that it almost glowed, the three white feathers sparkled, and the only holes were the ones for his head and arms to go through. 'Nooooo!' he howled. 'What's happened to my beautiful shirt? That was history, that was! Gareth Edwards ripped those buttons off his very own self!'

Suddenly, Betsan knew exactly what had happened. She rubbed her fingers over the end of the stick, covering them in glittery stuff. Then she grabbed Maldwyn's bright red, brand new, hole free sleeve. In an instant the old tatty shirt was back.

The two stared at each other. Maldwyn's mouth was open.

'We've got to talk, Maldwyn,' Betsan said, and for once he didn't correct her.

'Come on,' Betsan led the way through the kissing-gate and out of the Rec. 'Let's go to my house. We can talk there. Mam's at work and Granch is playing bowls with Senior Citizens today. We can talk about things without getting interrupted, and back home we won't run into Crusher and Dwayne and –' she stopped, wishing her brain had been working properly, or she could call back the words or something.

Maldwyn ducked his head. 'You can say it,' he said, miserably. 'Get bullied. Oh, Bets, I wish I was bigger! I'd bash 'em until their teeth rattled. I'd make sure they didn't pick on anyone ever again.'

'Bashing them wouldn't work,' Betsan was certain about that. 'That would just make us as bad as them. They need to be taught a lesson, right, but not that one.'

'I s'pose so,' Maldwyn said. 'But I'd feel better! Anyway, never mind about them. What's going on with my shirt and stuff?'

'You aren't going to believe it,' Betsan said. 'But I think I've found a magic wand.'

'Pull the other one, Bets!' Maldwyn chortled, 'it's got bells on!'

'No, honest, Mal!' Betsan led the way through the archway and into the *gwli* that ran behind the terraced houses. She opened the garden door and they went in.

44

'Have some more chocolate,' she said, taking yet another bar from her jeans pocket. 'And another. And another. And another . . .'

Maldwyn's mouth had fallen open. 'You couldn't afford to buy all that, Betsan, and you aren't the sort of person to pinch it.'

'Have some more,' Betsan repeated, grinning and pulling out bar after bar after bar.

'Hang on,' Maldwyn stared at her jeans. 'Your pocket isn't big enough to hold all that chocolate!'

'At last, the penny's dropped!' Betsan said. 'Listen, will you? I found this stick thing up on the mountain. It fell out of a clear blue sky, bashed me on the head, and left this glittery stuff all over me.'

'Glittery stuff?' Maldwyn sounded bewildered.

Betsan rubbed her fingers over the end of the wand tucked down her trouser leg and held it out towards him. 'Glittery stuff,' she repeated. 'See?'

Maldwyn stared. 'What does it do?'

'Come down the raspberry bushes with me. You'll see.'

Chapter Seven

As the sky grew lighter, the magic orange lights (which were fixed right at the top of huge, tall poles) went out, one by one, although there was no wind to blow them. Gwydion stopped for a while and watched as the orange glow disappeared. It was amazing! One minute there a light was, glowing nice and steadily, the next – phoot! Gone! Fang sat patiently waiting while Gwydion watched the magically disappearing lights.

Then Gwydion heard a strange noise. It sounded like a whole army, clinking and clattering, coming round the corner. The last thing Gwydion wanted to meet (apart from another of the monsters with the fearsome glowing eyes) was an army on the march. Armies tended to scoop up strangers they met while marching, in case they were spies or something. And then they stuck them in smelly dungeons, while they decided if they were spies and if so, what they should do about it. Sometimes, deciding took years and years. Gwydion decided it was time to make himself scarce. Frantically looking about for a place to hide, he spotted an archway halfway down one of the long-houses, and he and Fang slipped inside. Gwydion, taking great care to stay hidden, peered out.

Around the corner came, not a long line of marching men, but a strange object, rather like the carts that carried goods and people around Ynys Haf. It had wheels, and it made a humming sound as well as the rattling and clinking, *but there was nothing pulling it along!* No horse, no ox, nothing. It just moved along on its own. Gwydion decided that somewhere close by there must be a very powerful magician. Only someone with really strong magic could have made the lights-on-poles and the cart-with-no-horse!

The back of the cart was full of white bottles, which were making the clinking sound. The cart's driver wore a strange, flat hat with a shiny visor sticking out to shade his eyes from the morning sun, rather like the helmet the King wore when he went to war. The magic cart kept stopping, and each time it rattled to a halt along the length of the long-house, the driver leapt off and left one or two or three of the bottles outside a door. Then he would pick up any empty bottles left outside the doors, and dump them in bright red boxes at the back of the cart. Then, in he'd jump again, and the cart would rattle a little further along the black road. Fang (who had probably seen a great many milk-floats in his time and was rather bored) yawned.

When Gwydion was certain that the strange cart-with-no-horse had completely disappeared, and he'd waited a little longer to make sure another one wasn't on its way round the corner, he set off down the road. He wasn't really sure what to do now. He hadn't found Merlin's wand, but this place (whenever he was) seemed much more dangerous than Ynys Haf, and he was beginning to get definitely nervous. Not *scared* exactly, but certainly a bit jumpy. Should he give up, go back up the mountain, find the Time Door stones again and go home, or keep looking? He was tempted to turn round and go back, but back home was Merlin, and he was going to be doubly cross with Gwydion, not only because he still hadn't found the wand, but because by now Merlin would certainly know that Gwydion had slipped through a Door. No, before he went back, Gwydion needed to find that wand. Whatever horrors this Time held in store for him, he had no choice but to stay.

'Come on, Fang!' he said. They kept walking, away from the mountain road. People were beginning to appear from the many doors in the long-houses, and some of them stared curiously at Gwydion and Fang. Gwydion soon realised this was because, compared to everyone else, his clothes looked rather strange. No one else seemed to be wearing leather jerkins and tight leggings here, let alone hobnail boots with curly tops. He slipped into another of the arched doorways, and concentrated hard on a New Clothes Spell. Most of the men and boys seemed to be wearing blue trousers and light-and-dark striped shoes and short-sleeved, round-necked tunic things. The air around Gwydion shimmered, and instantly he was wearing an identical outfit. No one except Fang had seen him change his clothes, and, apart from sneezing when the magic tickled his nose, Fang didn't seem to worry much about his new master's changed appearance.

They set off in search of Merlin's wand. It seemed to Gwydion that it was no use wandering around this strange town trying to guess where it might be. He could be here until he was three hundred if he did that. No, what he needed to do was find a quiet spot, sit down and try to concentrate on *feeling* where the wand was. With magic as strong as the wand had, surely he should be able to sense it, somehow, if it was fairly close.

'If you were an Ynys Haf hound, Fang,' he said, ruffling the dog's ears, 'you'd be leading me to it, no problem. Ynys Haf dogs can sniff out magic at 200 paces.' The dog gave him a look which said, "in your dreams, mate." The less Fang had to do with that fizzy stuff which made him sneeze, the better, as far as he was concerned. Besides, it was long past breakfast time, and he was hungry. He had usually been fed by now, and although his old master (this strange boy was most certainly his new one) kept him short of food, a little food was better than none. He put his large paw firmly on Gwydion's knee and looked up. He concentrated hard, looked Gwydion straight in the eye and thought "Food, please? Food? Food?"

Gwydion frowned. 'Do you know, Fang, boy, I think it's time we found something to eat.' The dog whined. Obviously this strange boy was quite intelligent for a human. Perhaps, even though Gwydion had only two legs and no tail, Fang might be able to train him to be quite useful, given time.

Gwydion looked carefully around him. There was no one about. He wiggled his hands, cracked his knuckles, and suddenly, on the floor in front of the dog was a large bowl full of meat. Fang sniffed. Beef! This was better than Pricerite Doggichunks! His tail wagging, he put his nose down and began to eat. Gwydion, in whose hands a large, hot, roast chicken had magically appeared, joined him, and when they had finished eating they refreshed themselves with water and blackberry juice cordial.

It was fully light now, and people were bustling around. They weren't staring at Gwydion any more, now that he was wearing the same clothes as everyone else, but some of the older people gave him curious looks, perhaps because they didn't recognise him. Although the kingdom was extremely rich, it was probably quite small, and Gwydion realised that people would easily pick out a stranger. In some kingdoms being a stranger was enough to get you locked up somewhere deep and dark, usually with rats, but here the looks seemed friendly, so Gwydion wasn't worried. He went round a corner, and found that the road led uphill. Fang at his heels, he decided to see where it went, still trying to "feel" if the wand was anywhere about.

At the top of the hill was a curious semi-circular gate leading into a green field. There were a lot of people in the middle of the field, where someone had marked a pattern of lines inside a painted rectangle on the ground. Half the people inside the painted lines were dressed in blue tunics and short trousers, the other half dressed in yellow ones. They seemed to be having a fight, and Gwydion began to walk quickly up towards the field. Perhaps they were fighting over the wand!

When he got close, he saw that it wasn't the wand at all. They appeared to be wrestling in heaps around an oval brown object. Sometimes they kicked it, sometimes they carried it, and sometimes just one person would pick it up and run very fast towards some H-shaped posts stuck in the ground, one set at each end. It was very strange, but they seemed to be having fun, not fighting, especially when they were all rolling around on the ground. There was a lot of shouting coming from some people who were watching, and Gwydion realised that the people in the middle of the field were having some kind of tournament, although the rules seemed very hard to make out. Jousting was much easier, he thought. For jousting, all you needed to do was climb on a horse and ride very fast towards the other person and try to poke him off his own horse with your lance. If you did, and the other person landed – splat! – on the seat of his armour, you won. Simple! But this game – it was very, very strange.

Standing close beside him was a short, slim person of about his own age, dressed in blue trousers and a round-necked, brightly coloured tunic, just like his own. Although the person was wearing boys' clothes, it looked very much like a girl. Next to her stood a taller, thin person, wearing a bright red shirt with three white feathers on the front. The shirt was very tattered. Gwydion wasn't sure what had drawn his attention to these two: they were having some sort of very earnest conversation, their heads close together, their faces looking worried. And then Gwydion realised what had caught his eye.

The girl had sparkle on her fingers.

Chapter Eight

She had the wand then. Or at least knew where it was. When the boy and girl left the field, Gwydion followed them. They went back down the hill towards the long-houses, and through one of the archways that Gwydion had hidden in to watch the cart-without-a-horse and to change his clothes. Gwydion waited a while and then followed, Fang at his heels, peering carefully around the corner to see where the two had gone. They were in a little garden, on a square of grass, eating squares of dark brown stuff as they talked, their heads close together so Gwydion couldn't overhear what they were saying. The garden was laid out in neat rows of cabbages, lettuces, and fruit bushes, and in one corner was a little hut made entirely of glass, filled with plants covered in large, strange, red fruit. The two got up from the grass and started towards the fruit bushes at the end of the garden. Suddenly, Gwydion let out a shout of alarm. The girl's blue and white shoes were flashing with bright red, blinking eyes! She had a dragon in her shoes! He had to rescue her! What if the dragon got out and ate her, and she knew where the wand was? That would be terrible. He'd never get it back then.

'Stop!' he yelled, and hurled himself at her back, knocking her to the ground.

Gwydion sat on her, grabbed her feet, ripped off her shoes, and flung them into the air. One of them landed in a flower bed, the other sailed through one of the panes in the glass house with a crashing, tinkling noise. Fang enthusiastically joined in the wonderful new game, grabbing hold of the girl's trouser-leg and shaking it, growling loudly.

'Cut that out!' the girl shouted, pulling her leg away from the dog. 'What do you think you're doing with my trainers, you dope?' She glared angrily at Gwydion.

'Your shoes are evil, my lady!' Gwydion gasped. 'I saw the dragon's eyes blinking at me. At any moment it might have leapt out and eaten you up entirely.'

'Du-uh!' the girl said scornfully. 'Haven't you ever seen trainers with flashing lights before?'

Gwydion suddenly realised that he had not only shown himself to one of this Time's people, he had also made a bit of a fool of himself. 'N-no,' he stammered. 'Actually, my lady, I haven't.'

The girl stared at him, and then at the dog. The boy was looking at it, too.

'Hey, Betsan,' he said suddenly. 'Isn't that Crusher's father's rottweiler? The savage one, that snarls and barks whenever we walk past the scrap yard? Fang?'

Fang, hearing his name, looked up and wagged his tail.

'Yes,' Gwydion said. 'Fang wasn't very happy there. He had a bad temper, and rather a nasty nature, so I – um.' He wasn't quite sure how to tell these strange people that he had magicked the savageness away. Dogs weren't meant to be savage: this dog had been wrongly treated to make him so unfriendly. It was a terrible thing to treat an animal badly. Unless it was a dragon trying to eat you, of course. Then you were allowed to kill it, first.

Suddenly he remembered the girl's glitter-coated fingertips and decided this might be a good time to change the subject. 'I couldn't help noticing,' he began, 'you seem to have some – er, stuff – on your fingers.'

The girl opened out her hand and looked. 'Yes, I have. I was just explaining to Maldwyn about the chocolate and all that other weird stuff, and –.' She stared at Gwydion. 'What do you know about it?'

Gwydion looked uncomfortable. 'Well, it comes from a magi– From a wa– Well, it belongs to Mer–' He stopped. Because he didn't know where – or when – he was, he didn't know how much these people would understand about Merlin, and magic and things. They must certainly have heard of Merlin. Everyone knew about Merlin, wherever they went in the kingdom. Merlin was the most famous wizard of all.

Betsan got up from the grass, awkwardly, as if her leg was stiff. She lifted up her tunic, and unbuckled the belt of her trousers, slipping off a loop of cord. Then, slowly, she pulled at the cord – and from down her trouser-leg appeared Merlin's missing wand!

'You've got it!' Gwydion said, joyfully. She had the wand. He wondered if he could snatch it and run like mad up the mountain towards the Time Door. Maldwyn must have guessed what was going through his mind, though.

'Don't even think about it,' he warned. 'I'm gonna play full-back one day, like my Uncle Gethin, and I can tackle you and bring you down no problem. I'm like lightnin', me.'

Gwydion wasn't sure what he was talking about, but he sighed and gave in.

'It's mine,' the girl said, frowning. 'I found it! Finder's keepers!'

'I beg your pardon, lady.' Gwydion felt cross. 'But that wand is my teacher's. It is Merlin's, and no one else's.'

'Merlin?' the girl whispered, her eyes very round. '*The* Merlin?'

Gwydion stood very tall, and the dog stood with him. 'There is only one Merlin, Master of All Amazing and Magical Mysteries, and this is his wand. Which he lost,' he added. 'So will you give it back to me, please?'

Maldwyn was still staring at him. 'Is that why my shirt went all horrible and new?' he asked.

'I don't know about that, but sometimes the wand does what it wants. Merlin can control it, but only if he's quite close. Which at the moment, he isn't,' Gwydion finished. 'I wish he were, because then he'd show you . . .'

'Ooh, don't wish for anything, please!' the girl said, hurriedly. 'Some seriously weird stuff has been happening around here since I found that thing up on the Graig, I can tell you.' She shivered, and suddenly seemed to make up her mind. 'I don't want the wand thing. It's scary. Only –' she frowned, looking at Gwydion hard, and put the hand with the wand behind her back. 'Only, if it's Merlin's wand, and you've come to get it, who are you? And where do you come from? How do I know you will give it back to him?'

Gwydion thought, quickly. He couldn't explain to these people about the Time Door. Ordinary people weren't magic. They might understand about some things, but not about the Time Doors. Besides, what would happen if one of them took it into their head to try to travel through a Door? That would be horribly dangerous, and Merlin wouldn't like that one bit. Anything might happen if mortals started popping in and out of Time like rabbits in a warren.

'Well, firstly, my name is Gwydion. And I'll tell you what,' he said, craftily. 'Give me the wand. I'll take care of it.' It wasn't very honest, but it seemed to be the only safe way out of his problems.

'You must be joking!' Betsan said. 'If I give you the wand, we'll never see you again, right? You'd do a runner. Or disappear somehow.'

Gwydion had to agree, although he didn't say so. That was exactly what he'd had in mind. 'All right. You keep it. Give it back when you've decided. Only you must give it back. Or I'm in dead trouble, honest,' he finished.

'Let me think about it,' Betsan said carefully. 'Where can we meet?'

'Up on the mountain. At nightfall.'

The trouble was, Gwydion didn't trust these strangers any more than they trusted him. True, they had said that they would meet him and give back the wand, but he knew perfectly well that people who weren't used to magic the way he was, got silly and excited just by the idea of it. They didn't realise how hard it was to control and how dangerous it could be. Just when you thought you had magic all sorted out, and were in charge of it, it turned on you when you were least expecting it. It was rather like getting a furious dragon by the tail. While you were holding tightly to one end, the other end was likely to turn round and bite your head off.

No, he decided. He wouldn't go up the mountain and wait for them. He'd hang around this longhouse and make sure they didn't go anywhere else, taking the wand with them. And if they hadn't come out by sundown, he'd go in and get the wand somehow. Steal it, if he had to. It wasn't theirs, after all. He looked around him, looking for a place to hide. There was a small wooden building next to the long-house, with two doors. He opened the first one and peered inside. Inside was a heap of black, glittery stuff, like a pile of jagged stones. He put out a hand and touched it. It was very dirty. His hand was covered in black. He wiped the black off on his tunic and closed the door. Much too dirty to hide in. He'd leave tracks behind him wherever he went. He opened the next door. Inside, it was very strange: a huge, white vase thing with an oval wooden frame stood in the middle of the floor. A metal box was fixed high up on the wall behind it, and a chain with a round handle dangled from it, a bit like the doorbell outside Merlin's tower. Without thinking who – or what – might be summoned by the sound of the bell, Gwydion grabbed the handle and pulled. He shot straight out of the door in alarm as a waterfall cascaded into the vase from nowhere! First people in a box, now a waterfall in a vase! Whatever next! He didn't think he wanted to hide in there, either. What if the waterfall overflowed and washed him away?

Perhaps there was somewhere he could hide inside the long-house . . .

Chapter Nine

Fang close at his heels, Gwydion tiptoed to the door of the house. It had a pane of clear glass set into it, and curtains of white cloth so fine that they looked like mist hanging across the glass. He could just see into the room. It was empty, except for a table and some chairs. There were other things in the room that he didn't recognise, but nothing that looked magical, or as if it might attack him, so as softly as he could he pressed down on the handle of the door and crept inside. The floor was made of shiny blue and yellow tiles, and Gwydion didn't notice that his shoes, which had been investigating the coal-hole next to the *tŷ bach*, had left black footprints wherever he walked.

He stood next to the table and listened. He could hear voices in another room, but otherwise the house was silent. He looked around him. There was a large box with four round things on the top of it. He couldn't imagine what it was for. Next to it was another box with a round door: he knelt down and peered inside. It was half-full of crumpled clothes. Some sort of strange cupboard, then. Not much good for keeping clothes tidy, though: they were all jumbled up. Another, taller box stood next to that. Gwydion took hold of the handle and pulled. He leapt backwards in alarm. Somewhere around there was definitely a powerful wizard. He'd suspected it all along, and now he was certain. Somehow these people had managed to trap winter inside the box! The air inside it steamed with cold. It was freezing, and the inside of the box glowed like the sun. The big box was full of stuff – jars and bottles and packages – stacked on its shelves, but Gwydion didn't wait to find out what was in them. They were almost certainly magical potions, and he didn't want to spend long around *that* sort of thing. He shut the door, quick, in case the winter escaped or the spells attacked him. Spells did that, sometimes.

Cautiously he opened the door of the room. There was a little passageway outside, a door leading off it and a flight of stairs going upward. Beneath the stairs there was a small door. Gwydion silently opened it and slipped inside. It was dark, and smelled strange and dusty, but at least it didn't have winter or magic in it. This would do as a place to wait. He closed the door behind him and, Fang by his side, settled down on the floor in the darkness.

He must have slept for a while, because the sound of shouting woke him up. He sat up, bashed his head on something, and saw stars. The shouting was coming from outside. He heard the girl's voice – what had the boy called her? – oh yes, Betsan.

She sounded upset, and he heard the boy, too. There were other older, louder, rougher voices.

Beside him Fang stiffened. Gwydion dropped his hand to the dog's head and felt the fur rising stiffly on the back of its neck. 'Shh!' he whispered, and one hand firmly on the dog's collar, he silently opened the door.

The shouting was coming from the garden place outside the longhouse. Gwydion crept to the door and peered through the filmy curtains. Betsan and the boy were there, but also some bigger boys. One of the big boys was holding Betsan, the other was holding the boy who wore the little round windows on his nose.

'You've got no right to come in our garden, Dwayne Morris!' Betsan shrieked. 'Let me go! And Crusher, you let Maldwyn go, too, or else . . .'

'Or else what?' the boy called Crusher sneered. 'What are you gonna do about it, small fry?'

'I'll tell –'

The boy holding her laughed. It wasn't a nice laugh. 'Who? Your Mam? Fat chance she'd do anything. Your grandpa? Puff of wind'd blow 'im over. Your Dad?' He looked all round him, pretending to be scared. 'Ooh, I'm terrified, me! Last I heard, your Dad was about a thousand miles away, right? So what's 'e gonna do, eh?' And he gave Betsan's arm a painful twist. Gwydion was impressed to see that she didn't yell or cry. She was brave, that one. The boy Maldwyn, though, also struggled and fought against the one called Crusher, but he was so small that Crusher just held on and didn't take any notice.

'Let Maldwyn go. I've got some money. Just go away and leave us alone.'

'Money, eh? How much?' Crusher asked.

'About five pounds.'

'Don't give them anything, Betsan!' Maldwyn yelled, renewing his efforts to struggle free.

'We could just take the money,' Dwayne said, grinning evilly, 'and lock 'em up in the coal 'ole. That'd be good, wouldn't it, Crush?' And he began to drag Betsan towards the doors near the house.

'Why don't you let her go?' Gwydion's voice was low and pleasant, but both the bullies heard it.

'I thought I heard something squeak, then,' Dwayne said, cupping his hand over his ear. 'How about you, Crush?'

But Crusher was staring at Fang. ''Ere!' he said. 'That's my dog! What you doin' with it?'

'Your dog, is it?' Gwydion replied, still holding Fang's collar. Fang growled, deep in his chest. Gwydion could feel the rumble travelling through his fingers. 'Want it back?'

' Of course I do, thick-'ead. It's a valuable dog, that! My old man trained that dog up from a pup. It's a killer, that dog! 'It'll 'ave your throat out soon as look at you!'

'Right.' And Gwydion let go of Fang's collar. He had expected the dog to bound forward and attack the big boys, but instead, it moved forward slowly on stiff legs, its head lowered, its teeth bared. Fascinated, the boys watched it, and then Crusher said 'Here, boy! Come on, you ugly brute. Heel!'

Fang, still walking slowly towards them, gave Crusher a look which suggested that if he should get close to Crusher's heel, he would certainly bite it off. Crusher began to look a bit nervous, then got the message that was showing in Fang's eyes and began to back away. Then he turned and began to run, closely followed by Dwayne. They just made it to the apple tree at the end of the garden, and both of them tried to climb it at once. Fang got a good snap at Dwayne's rear end (he was a slower runner than Crusher) before Dwayne managed to get out of the reach of his flashing teeth.

Gwydion stood under the tree, looking up. 'If you ever bother either of these people again, you'll be sorry,' he said quietly. 'Just remember that, right?'

Crusher felt braver now that he was out of Fang's reach. 'That's still my dog, that is. I'm gonna get the coppers on you for stealing my dog.'

Gwydion tugged Fang's ear, gently, then put his hand firmly on the dog's head. 'Whose dog are you, Fang?'

It was what happened next that convinced Dwayne AND Crusher that Gwydion was no ordinary boy, and that he meant business.

Fang stood up on his hind legs, rested his front

paws against the apple tree, and looked up at his former master. 'I'm HIS dog,' he said. His voice was sort of woofly, but perfectly clear. 'And if you ever lay hands on people smaller than you, or kick another dog, or starve another dog, or beat another dog, I'll come and bite you up into little pieces. And then I'll bite you again.'

Even Maldwyn had to smile at the look of mingled horror and amazement on their faces.

Then Gwydion took hold of Fang's collar, and held it. 'Get down from that tree and go,' he said sternly. Fang growled in agreement.

Slowly (and only after thinking about it for a bit) Crusher and Dwayne climbed down. Dwayne clutched the seat of his jeans, which had a large tear in them. His boxer shorts (which were covered in pink bunnies because his Mam had bought them for him for Christmas) stuck out of the rip. Neither boy took his eyes off Gwydion and the dog. In fact they walked backwards out of the garden gate, bumped into the wall, and as soon as they felt it was safe, began to run.

Chapter Ten

When Gwydion turned round, Betsan was right behind him. She put her arms round him and gave him a hug, then did the same to Fang, who washed her face with his slobbery tongue.

'Thanks, Gwydion,' she said. 'I'm not even going to ask what you were doing, hiding in our house, but thanks anyway for rescuing us.'

'Yeah, thanks,' Maldwyn mumbled, but Gwydion could tell that the boy was still unhappy. He thought he could understand, a little bit, why. He had wanted to protect Betsan himself, and hadn't been able to.

'Look,' Gwydion began. 'I'm bigger and older than you, and I had Fang, right? If you'd had a dog like him, you could have chased them up the tree, too.'

'No I couldn't,' Maldwyn said miserably. 'With my luck the dog would have bitten me, not them. I'll never be any good. I'm too small and skinny. And I wear glasses. I'm fed up with people picking on me all the time.'

Gwydion looked thoughtful. 'Then we'll make sure they don't do it any more.'

Maldwyn stared. 'Oh, yeah? How are we going to do that? I'm not going to put my underpants on over my trousers and turn into Superman overnight, am I?'

Gwydion didn't understand what he meant. 'Suppose I teach you a thing or two?' he suggested. 'Then you could handle anything that came your way.'

'What are you going to teach me?' Maldwyn asked. 'Karate? Judo? I'll still be little, won't I?'

Gwydion shook his head. 'I don't know what those things are,' he said, 'sorry and all that. But I could teach you a bit of magic.'

Maldwyn's eyes, became as round as his glasses. 'You *what*?' he said, disbelievingly. 'Oh, pull the other one, mate. There's no such thing as magic.'

Betsan got exasperated. 'Oh, for goodness sake, Maldwyn!'

'Elliott,' the boy said automatically, shoving his glasses up his nose. 'I'm Elliott.'

'No you aren't,' Betsan said fiercely, 'you're Maldwyn, and you're my friend, and I think you're great. Even if you aren't big, with huge muscles like Arnold whatsisname. And Gwydion *can* do magic. I mean, have you ever heard a dog talk before?'

Maldwyn, who had turned pink with embarrassment, shrugged. 'Could have been throwing his voice, couldn't he? Like a ventroquilly– ventryquo– oh, you know, one of those people who make dolls talk.'

'But he's not a ventriloquist, are you, Gwydion? Your magic is real, isn't it. I know it is, because I found the wand, didn't I?'

Gwydion nodded, slowly. 'It's real, Betsan. And magic is dangerous, but I can show Maldwyn just enough to make sure no one will ever bully him again.'

'Then show him!' Betsan begged. 'I'll give you the wand, then, and you can go back to wherever you came from.'

Gwydion beamed. 'All right. I was going to show him anyway, but yes, I'll do it in exchange for the wand. But Maldwyn –'

Maldwyn was watching Gwydion as if he expected him to turn blue and fly away. 'Yes?'

'Don't ever use what I tell you to harm anyone else, promise? Because magic will always turn on people who try to use it wrongly. You must only use it on someone who is threatening you. Or Betsan,' he added.

Maldwyn nodded hard enough to make his glasses slither down his nose again. 'Promise. Honest, I won't.'

Gwydion put his arm round Maldwyn's skinny shoulders and whispered in his ear. Maldwyn closed his eyes and muttered something under his breath. Then he opened his eyes. He was grinning. It was a huge grin, a Christmas morning sort of grin, a Happy Birthday sort of grin, and behind the round glasses, his eyes were shining.

'Will you give me the wand now?' Gwydion asked. The quicker he got the wand, the faster he could be away from this Time and back to Merlin.

'It's upstairs. I'll just go up and get it –' Betsan began, and then stopped.

'Oh, hi, Granch! Bowls game over?'

'It is indeed, my lovely girl, and we won. Champions of the valley, that's us.' The old man looked at Gwydion. 'And here's a new face. Who might you be, young man?'

'I'm Gwydion, Sire.' Betsan's grandfather was staring at him, blue eyes bright under the bushy white eyebrows. Merlin would look like this old man, in another thousand years or so.

'Sire? Duw, there's polite!' the old man laughed. 'I like this boy, Betsan! He can come and see us again.' He patted Gwydion's shoulder, stooped to ruffle Fang's fur, and went into the house.

'I can't go and get the wand now, Gwydion,' Betsan said. 'Granch will want to know what I'm doing, and I can't lie to him. I'll meet you on the Graig, all right? At sunset tonight. I promise we'll be there, and I'll bring the wand.'

Gwydion frowned, but he understood. He was stuck here until sundown then. He decided to go up the mountain and wait. 'There are three stones,' he said. 'Two side by side, one on top of the other two. They – well, they aren't usually there, but if you follow the stream up the mountain, right to the top, there are three mountain ash trees close

69

together, and a little hollow. I'll meet you by there, all right?'

Betsan nodded. 'I think I know where you mean. Just before it gets dark then, I promise.'

Gwydion climbed the mountain to wait for Betsan and Maldwyn. It was a long wait, and the sun was hot, but he had Fang to keep him company. He decided to take the dog back with him when he went. He'd always wanted a dog, and this one was a beauty. He'd never seen one quite like it before, not in Ynys Haf.

As the sun began to slither down the western sky, turning it as pink as a rose, Gwydion could see, far down the valley, Maldwyn and Betsan climbing up the mountain they called Y Graig. When they came closer, he could see that Betsan had the wand in her hand. He flopped onto the rough grass, to wait for them to join him, and Fang rested his head on Gwydion's knee, his brown eyes sleepy in the heat. At last, Maldwyn and Betsan collapsed beside him. Maldwyn fanned his face with his hand and Betsan lay stretched out, her eyes closed. Gwydion wished they would give him the wand and let him go.

Without opening her eyes, Betsan said 'Tell us how you got here, Gwydion. Neither of us can really believe anything that has happened – the wand, the talking dog, the rugby shirt – all that magic and stuff. Please?'

So, bit by bit, Gwydion told them the whole story of Merlin, and the wand, and the Time Door.

Half way through Betsan was sitting up, and Maldwyn was hardly breathing with excitement.

'You mean,' Betsan said slowly when he'd finished, 'that on the Graig, there's a Door thingy that you can go through – and end up somewhere else?'

'Somewhen else,' Gwydion corrected her. 'You can go forward or back in Time. But,' he added, thinking that a warning might be a good idea, because Betsan was obviously very brave and brave people sometimes did stupid things, 'it would be very dangerous for you to try it. You might arrive on the other side and walk straight into a dragon or something. Very nasty. It'd burn you up soon as look at you.'

Betsan shuddered. 'I don't think either of us want to try to follow you, Gwydion.'

'I might,' Maldwyn said. 'I'm brave, now. I've got the bit of magic Gwydion gave me.'

'You've got to promise, Elliott!' Betsan said urgently. 'Promise you won't do it? I don't care how brave you are.'

'It's Maldwyn. Not Elliott, or Clint, or Jason or anything. Just Maldwyn.' Maldwyn said, and grinned. 'O.K., I promise.'

Betsan smiled. 'Here, Gwydion. Take the wand.' She handed it over, and Gwydion took it, thankfully. At last, the wand was his again. Well, Merlin's. All he had to do now was get it safely back.

Neither Gwydion nor Maldwyn had noticed that *Betsan* hadn't promised anything at all . . .

A few moments later, Betsan and Maldwyn watched as Gwydion stepped between the upright stones on top of the mountain. The air between them shimmered, and Gwydion didn't come out the other side. They peered between the stones, careful not to step inside the shimmery air. Gwydion had completely disappeared.

'That's that, then!' Maldwyn said. 'Not that anyone would ever believe us if we told them, Betsan.'

Betsan didn't answer. She was thinking about next Saturday, when she might – just *might,* mind, nothing definite – try walking between those stones herself.

But the strange thing was that, when she went up the Graig the next Saturday, she couldn't find the stones. Not anywhere.